Puddington's

Busy Day

Paddington's
MICHAEL BOND
Busy Day

Illustrated by R.W. Alley

Collins
An imprint of HarperCollins*Publishers*

One morning, Paddington looked out of his
bedroom window and saw that it was raining
outside.

He was very disappointed. He had planned
to spend the day in the garden and now he had
nothing to do.

"How about doing some painting?" suggested
Judy. "You can borrow my box of paints
if you like."

"There's a bowl of fruit in the other room,"
said Mrs Brown. "Why don't you try
painting that?"

"That should keep him
quiet for a while,"
said Mr Brown, as
Paddington left
the room.

But Paddington was back in no time at all. He held up the bowl of fruit for everyone to see.

"I've painted it blue so that it will match the wallpaper," he said.

"I have a feeling it is going to be one of those days," groaned Mrs Bird. "Has anyone else got any good ideas?"

"You could help Mrs Bird in the kitchen," said Mrs Brown.

"How about tidying up the loft?" said Mrs Bird hastily.

"Your stamps need putting into an album," said Jonathan.

"If you have any paste left over," said Judy, "you could stick lots of things together and make a collage like the one on the wall."

Paddington thought for
a moment.

"I think I'll start in
the kitchen," he said.
"I may make some
pastry. Bears like pastry."

"I think it's time I went to
the office," said Mr Brown.

Paddington was
soon hard at work
making pastry.

He used over
half a bag of flour
and he ended up
with most of it over
himself.

"You'd better go
upstairs and have a
wash," said Mrs Bird,
"or you will end up
looking like a polar
bear."

"I do hope it stops
raining soon," said Mrs
Brown.

On his way upstairs, Paddington remembered his stamps. His Aunt Lucy, who lived in the Home for Retired Bears in Lima, was always sending him postcards.

He collected them all into a big pile and took them along to the bathroom so that he could get the stamps off with the water at the same time as he washed.

But as soon as the water started mixing with the flour, it turned into paste, and in no time at all he found he had more stamps stuck to his duffle coat than in his album.

Paddington decided it might be a good time to try his paw at tidying the loft. At least no one would be able to see him up there.

He made himself some marmalade sandwiches and found his torch. Then he climbed up the special folding ladder Mr Brown used for going into the roof.

Paddington had never been in the loft before
and it was much darker than he had expected.

He hadn't gone very far when he
stepped on a loose board by
mistake.

   The other end came up
and hit him on the back
of the head.

               The torch went one way.
          The marmalade sandwiches
                    went another way.
                 And Paddington...

...went straight through his bedroom ceiling.
Back in his room, Paddington gazed up at
the hole.

"Oh dear," he said to the world in general.
"I think I'm in trouble again!"

He looked at himself sadly in the mirror,
wondering what to do next, and as he did so he
had an idea.

He fetched his pastry and the rest of the flour
from the kitchen. Then he collected Judy's
painting set and the rest of his stamps.
After that he found a bucket
and a large spoon
and some old
newspapers
and he set
to work.

The Browns could hardly believe their eyes when they saw what Paddington had been up to.

"I've never seen a collage on a ceiling before," said Judy.

"I wish I'd thought of it," said Jonathan.

"It looks good enough to eat," said Mrs Brown. "Whatever gave you the idea?"

"It came to me," said Paddington vaguely. "It's what's known as a ceilingage. I shall keep it there to remind me of all the things you can do on a rainy day."

"I think," said Mrs Bird, "rain or no rain,
it's high time you had a bath."
    And even Paddington had to
agree that was the best idea
he had heard so far
that day.

    "The trouble with having nothing to do," he
said, "is that you do get very sticky. Especially if
you happen to be a bear."